First Aladdin Paperbacks edition June 2003
Copyright © 2000 by Lisa Campbell Ernst

ALADDIN PAPERBACKS
An imprint of Simon & Schuster Children's Publishing Division
1230 Avenue of the Americas New York, NY 10020
Designed by Lisa Campbell Ernst.
The text of this book was set in Goudy Old Style.
The illustrations are rendered in pastel, ink, and pencil.
Manufactured in China
20 19 18 17 16 15 14
The Library of Congress has cataloged the hardcover edition as follows:
Ernst, Lisa Campbell. Goldilocks returns / written and illustrated by
Lisa Campbell Ernst.—1st ed. p. cm. Summary: Fifty years after
Goldilocks first met the three bears, she returns to fix up their
cottage and soothe her guilty conscience. ISBN 978-0-689-82537-8
[1. Bears—Fiction. 2. Humorous stories.] I. Title.
PZ7.E7323Go 2000 98-30099 CIP AC
ISBN 0-689-85705-5 (Aladdin pbk.)
ISBN-13: 978-0-689-85705-8 (Aladdin pbk.)
1215 SCP

for Allison

Goldilocks Returns

Lisa Campbell Ernst

Aladdin Paperbacks
New York London Toronto Sydney Singapore

As a child she was known as Goldilocks, and she was very naughty indeed. Her favorite hobby was snooping in houses where no one was at home—until, of course, all that dreadful trouble with the bears.

Then Goldilocks grew up, and the older she got the worse she felt about her *horrid* behavior. She shortened her name and pinned up her curls so no one would recognize her. Goldi opened a shop to help people protect themselves against snoops. But no matter how she tried to leave her life of crime behind, it haunted her day and night. Goldi had nightmares about bears. She cried at the mere sight of a teddy bear. Her customers even began to look like bears. "I can't take it any longer!" she sobbed at last. "It's time I set things right." Early one morning, Goldi loaded up her truck, turned her shop sign to CLOSED, and zoomed off toward the deep, dark woods.

At that very moment the three bears whom she had scared out of their wits years before were sitting down to breakfast.

They were Papa Bear, Mama Bear, and their son—who, though not a baby for some fifty years now, still went by the name Baby Bear. Due to the fright brought on by Goldilocks, he still had a wee little voice.

Their breakfast as usual was porridge, and as it had been every day since any of them could remember, it was much too hot to eat.

"Grab your hats." Papa Bear sighed, and the three unsuspecting bears left for their daily walk.

No sooner had the bears left than Goldi screeched to a stop in front of their cozy cottage. "It hasn't changed a bit," she gasped.

Strapping her tool belt on, Goldi walked to the door and knocked. A smile crept across her face as she realized the bears, again, were not at home.

Goldi walked right in.

"I'll fix *that*," she said, chuckling. With a drill in one hand, and a screwdriver in the other, Goldi swung into action.

Moments later the bears' door was laden with the finest in locking hardware: padlock, double bolt, and the secret antisnoop lock she used in only the most serious cases. "Won't they be delighted!" she crooned.

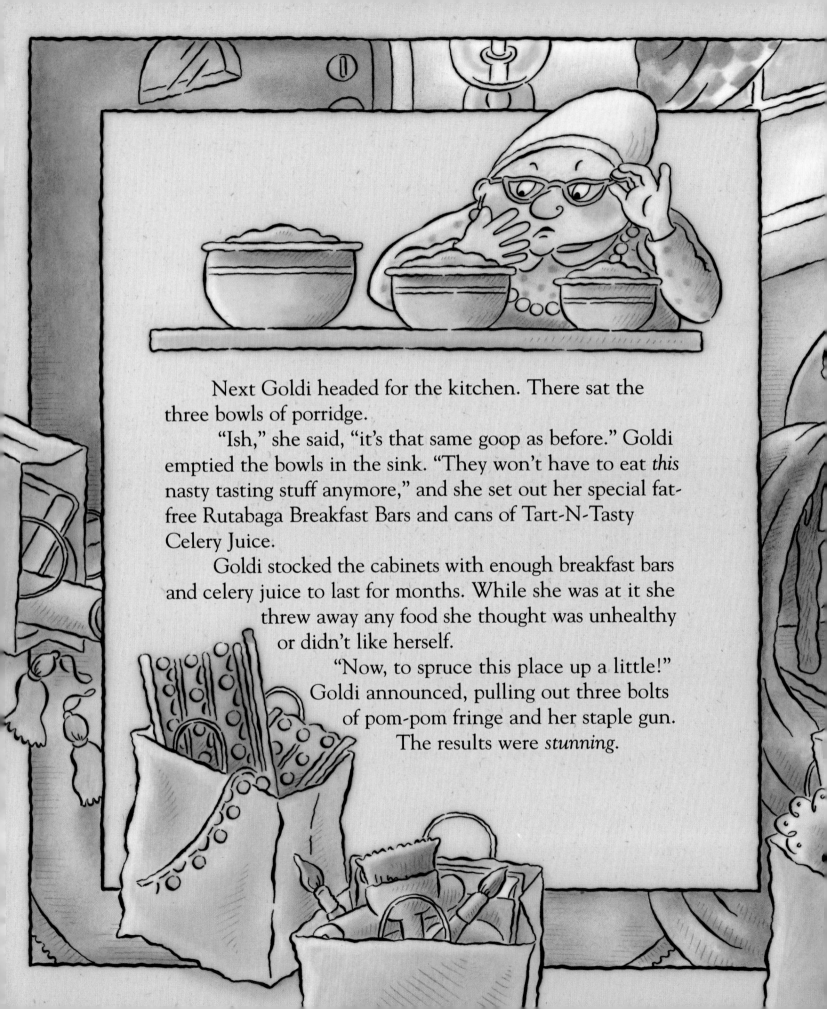

Next Goldi headed for the kitchen. There sat the three bowls of porridge.

"Ish," she said, "it's that same goop as before." Goldi emptied the bowls in the sink. "They won't have to eat *this* nasty tasting stuff anymore," and she set out her special fat-free Rutabaga Breakfast Bars and cans of Tart-N-Tasty Celery Juice.

Goldi stocked the cabinets with enough breakfast bars and celery juice to last for months. While she was at it she threw away any food she thought was unhealthy or didn't like herself.

"Now, to spruce this place up a little!" Goldi announced, pulling out three bolts of pom-pom fringe and her staple gun. The results were *stunning*.

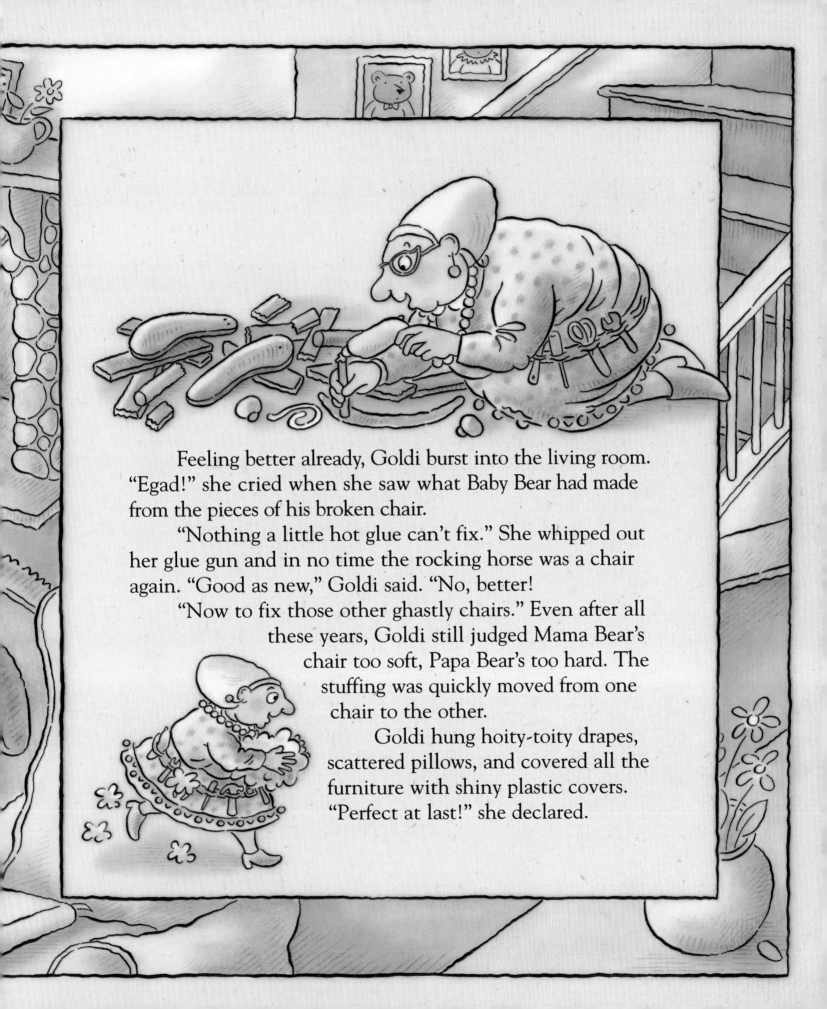

Feeling better already, Goldi burst into the living room. "Egad!" she cried when she saw what Baby Bear had made from the pieces of his broken chair.

"Nothing a little hot glue can't fix." She whipped out her glue gun and in no time the rocking horse was a chair again. "Good as new," Goldi said. "No, better!

"Now to fix those other ghastly chairs." Even after all these years, Goldi still judged Mama Bear's chair too soft, Papa Bear's too hard. The stuffing was quickly moved from one chair to the other.

Goldi hung hoity-toity drapes, scattered pillows, and covered all the furniture with shiny plastic covers. "Perfect at last!" she declared.

Goldi raced up the stairs to the three bears' bedroom. "Good gosh," she said, testing the beds of Papa Bear and Mama Bear, "just as I remembered: too hard, too soft." And before you could say Rip Van Winkle, she had adjusted the stuffings to her finicky liking.

Goldi sprayed Ravishing Roses perfume in the air and tied bouquets of plastic flowers around the room for a back-to-nature look.

"It's glorious!" Goldi sang, falling back on Baby Bear's bed to admire the room. "The bears will be so grateful."

Suddenly Goldi was exhausted, and once again, Baby Bear's bed was *just right*. Before she knew it, Goldi had drifted off to her most peaceful sleep in fifty years.

The bears, meanwhile, were finally returning home from their walk. Seeing the truck, they began to worry. They hadn't had much luck with visitors in the past.

"What on—" Papa Bear said, noticing the locks on the door. Then he heard Baby Bear squealing in the kitchen.

"Oh no! Oh my gosh! Oh my heavens!" he cried in his wee little voice. "Look! LOOK!"

With jaws dropping and eyes popping, the two older bears did just that.

Papa Bear snarled at the sight of the table, and bellowed in his big, deep voice, "Someone has taken my porridge!"

Mama Bear nodded. "Someone has taken *my* porridge," she said in her medium-size voice.

And Baby Bear, discovering the mess in the sink, cried in his wee little voice, "Someone has taken *my* porridge, and they've thrown it all away!"

Memory told the bears to race to the living room.

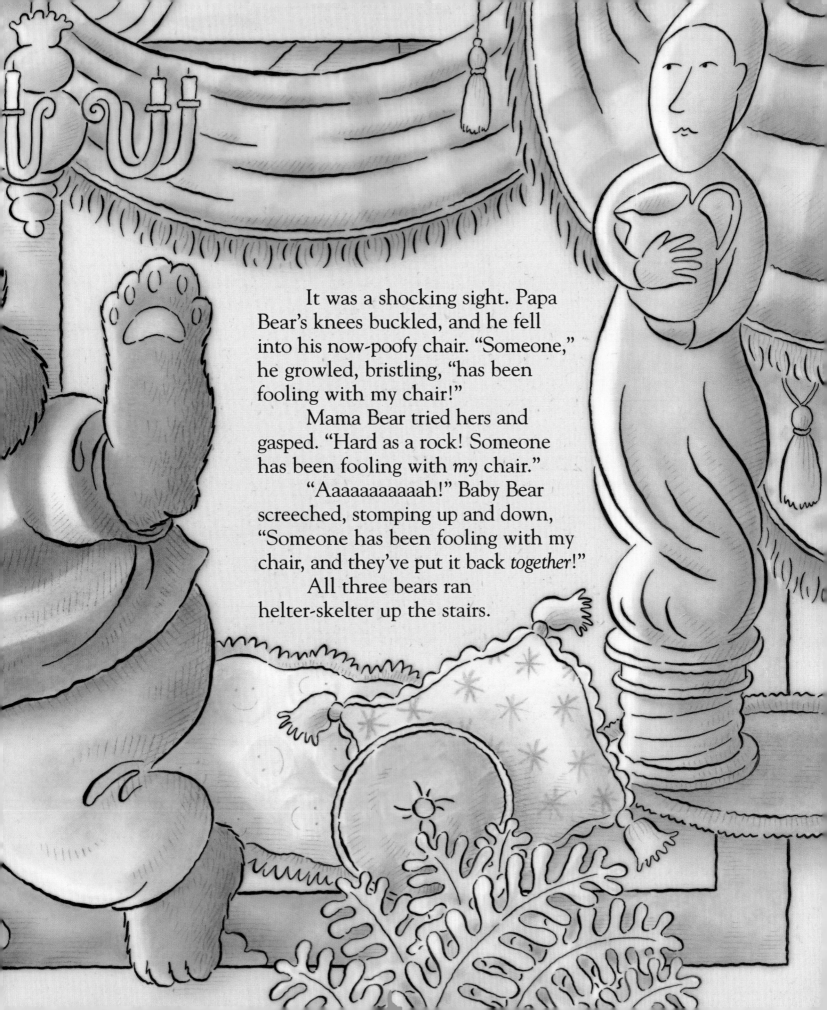

It was a shocking sight. Papa Bear's knees buckled, and he fell into his now-poofy chair. "Someone," he growled, bristling, "has been fooling with my chair!"

Mama Bear tried hers and gasped. "Hard as a rock! Someone has been fooling with *my* chair."

"Aaaaaaaaaaah!" Baby Bear screeched, stomping up and down, "Someone has been fooling with my chair, and they've put it back *together*!"

All three bears ran helter-skelter up the stairs.

"P-U!" Baby Bear gagged. "What's that smell?"

"Ravishing Roses," Mama Bear read, picking up the empty bottle from the floor.

The two older bears did not even check their beds— they *knew* where to look. What they saw made their fur stand on end.

Baby Bear began to tremble. "She's back!" he wailed, hoping it was all just a nightmare. "Someone's been sleeping in my bed, and here she is—*AGAIN*!"

And at that moment, Goldi's eyes popped open.

"You're home!" Goldi shouted, crushing each bear with a hug and kissing their furry cheeks. The shocked bears opened their mouths to protest, but Goldi raced on.

"Now, don't thank me. I know you're terribly grateful! But after all, I was the one who caused the trouble to begin with—of course I've more than made up for *that*."

Goldi gleefully danced through the house, pointing out her deeds. "Naturally I fixed that silly little chair," she said, "and got rid of that nasty porridge. The Rutabaga Breakfast Bars are fat free, so you might even be able to lose that extra weight there." She chuckled, tapping Papa Bear on the stomach.

A growl began to grow in Papa Bear's throat, but before he could get it out, Goldi tossed him the keys to her fancy locks, hugged them all again, climbed in her truck and was off.

"Wait! Come back!" yelled the bears, but it did no good. As her truck rounded a curve in the road, the bears saw a flash of gold—Goldi, smiling, unpinned her curls and shook them out in the breeze.

The dazed bears slowly turned back to their cottage. They moved awkwardly about their fancy-shmancy house. They couldn't eat, couldn't get comfortable in their chairs, and so finally went to bed.

No one slept a wink.

The next morning, the three exhausted bears sat at the kitchen table, miserably staring at their Rutabaga Breakfast Bars and celery juice. "Maybe we should go for a walk," Mama Bear suggested, and they all ran for their hats.

The three bears set off through the woods, relieved to be out of their house. But just then, Baby Bear spied something through the trees: It was a *very* mischievous looking little girl, skipping along the path that led straight to their cottage.

"Oh NO!" he panicked. "Not *this* again! We didn't lock the door! Quick! Stop her! She might eat our food! She might mess up the fancy things! She might break my chair!"

The bears began to run after the girl but then they suddenly stopped.

"Eat the food?" asked Mama Bear.

"Mess up the fancy things?" asked Papa Bear.

"Break my chair?" repeated Baby Bear.

Very slowly they all smiled.

And then, turning around, the
bears happily continued on their walk.

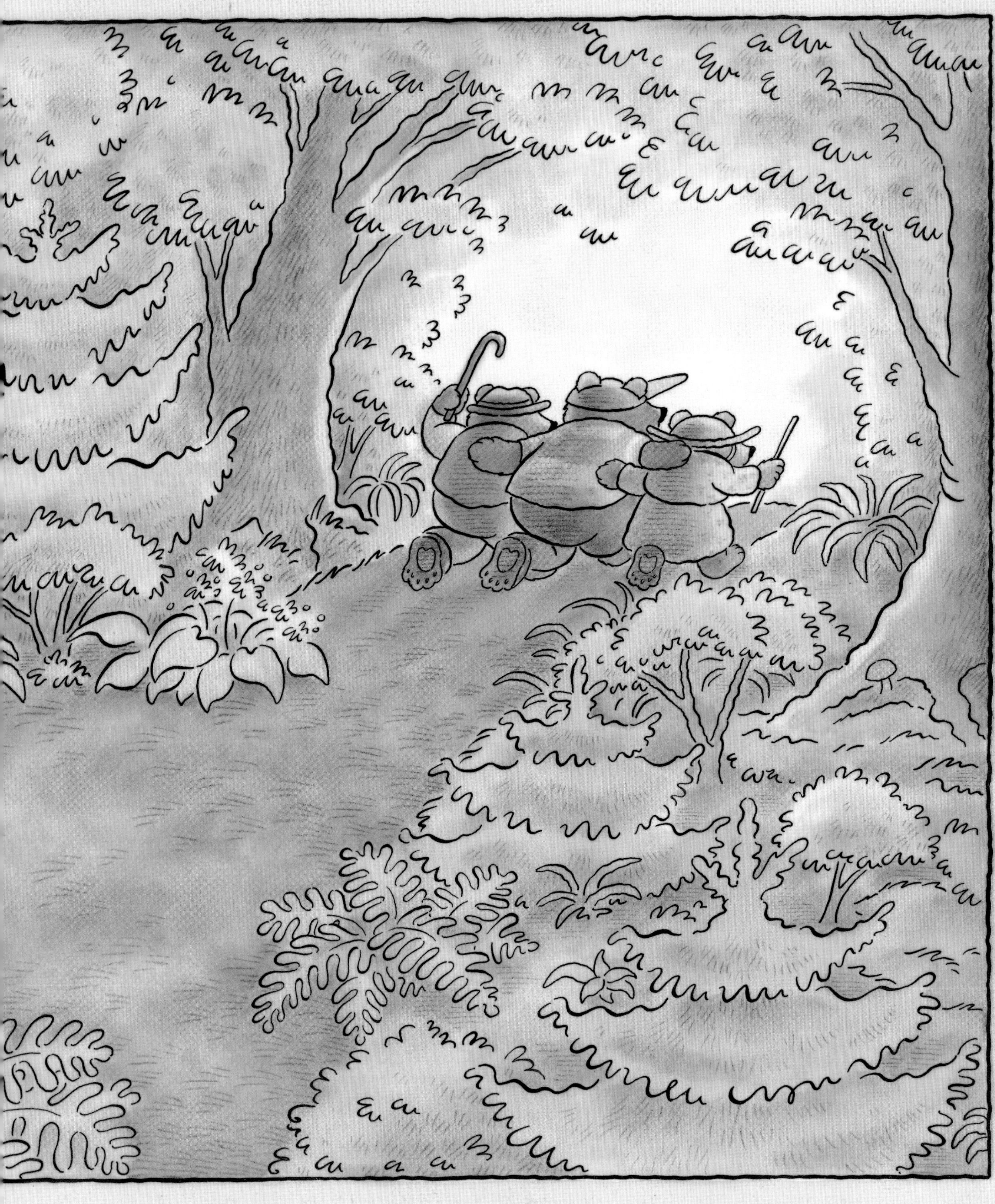